HENRY'S
Home Alone

Author
Brenda K. Dzierlinga

Illustrations by
Tabassum Hashmi

Henry's Home Alone

Author: Brenda K. Dzierlinga
Illustrator: Tabasum Hasmi
Editor: Brenda E. Cortez, Jean Sime
Layout: Michael Nicloy

Paperback ISBN-13: 979-8-9853960-5-8
Hardcover ISBN-13: 979-8-9853960-6-5

Published by BC Books LLC, Franklin, Wisconsin

HOWL
Help Others
With Love

BC BOOKS, LLC

Quantity and wholesale order requests can be emailed to:
brenda@bcbooksllc.com

Printed in The United States of America

To my Henry,

You made our home complete!

Love you,

Momma

"Good morning, Henry," Mom said, as she was greeted at her bedside. "It's a big day for you, let's go outside to potty and then have a nice breakfast!"

Henry barreled down the stairs, through the kitchen, and anxiously waited for his mom to catch up. There was a lot of new ground to explore at his new home and he was ready.

After Mom let Henry outside, she quickly woke Zack, Natalie, and Gavin to get ready for school. Henry came inside and found them all eating breakfast.

Zack was the first to finish his breakfast. "Mom, can I play with Henry for a bit before school?" he asked.

Mom nodded yes and said, "That is a great idea."

Shortly after, Mom gathered her purse and keys,
then turned to Henry.

"Come here Henry, it's time for me to go to work and
the kids must go to school," Mom said.
"Here is your bed," Don't worry, we will be back soon."

All of a sudden Henry was alone. Where did everyone go, he thought. Henry began to search the house for his new family.

He checked each bedroom, and looked out every window to see if he could find them.

Henry was sad. He wondered if they forgot him. Frantically, he searched for a way out of the house, but then he remembered Mom going out the back door.

Henry leaped through the screen door and was on his way to find them. He knew they had to be close, but which way did they go?

He started in the backyard, then made his way to the front. Feeling scared and confused, Henry started to walk around the block.

I will find them, he thought. *They are my family.*

Suddenly, there was a man standing next to a car with bright red and blue lights on. The man called Henry over.

"Here boy," he said. "It's not safe for you out here."

Henry walked to the man and was greeted with kindness.

"Let's find out where you belong." the officer said as he knelt down to check Henry's tag. "Oh, I see you belong to the family just a few blocks away. Get in, I will take you home."

After Henry was safe in the car, the officer called the number on the tag.

"Good morning, this is Officer Frank. Do you have a dog named Henry?" he questioned.

"Yes sir, we just adopted him two days ago. Is there something wrong with Henry?" Mom asked.

"I found him a few blocks away from your house, and I would like to bring him back for you." The officer replied.

Mom was shocked! She quickly responded, "I am at work, but I'll be right there."

As Mom pulled into the driveway, she saw the police car sitting in front of the house. She quickly made her way around the police car to see if it was really Henry.

"Oh, Henry, what happened?" Mom asked.

Henry looked sad and confused. As soon as he saw his mom, he jumped up to the barred window and cried with relief. He thought she forgot about him.

"Thank you Officer Frank," said Mom. "This was his first day alone at home. He must have been scared. I will take it from here."

Mom put a leash on Henry and walked him into the house. Together they sat on the floor.

"I'm sorry you were scared that we left." Mom explained to Henry. "You are part of our family now, we love you, and we will always come back for you."

Henry was relieved, but also exhausted from worrying and searching for his family. He laid down on his pillow and licked Mom's hand. As he drifted off to sleep, Mom pulled out of the driveway once again.

About the Author

About 12 years ago, Brenda and her daughter, Natalie, started a surprising journey together when they met Jerry and his sons, Zack and Gavin. Together, they blended into the perfect family, but yet it seemed something was missing. They adopted a dog to make their family complete. Little did they know how special this dog, Henry, would become to them, and others who enjoyed hearing his stories.

Brenda and her family live in a small town just outside of Madison, the capital of Wisconsin. She currently works in accounting, but her creative nature is an everyday hobby. Brenda enjoys wine tasting, flea markets, crafting, boating, camping and spending time with her family. Every month she gives herself a challenge of kindness and pays it forward. Giving back is truly special to Brenda, because after receiving her second chance at love, kindness, and family, she wants others to know that just the small things can make a difference.

Brenda's focus on this series is on second chances. They gave their dog Henry a second chance at nine years of age, and Brenda continues to adopt older animals. So many aging animals are overlooked for adoption most times, which is why Brenda will donate a percentage of book sales back to various humane societies to support the reduction of adoption fees for older animals.

CPSIA information can be obtained
at www.ICGtesting.com
Printed in the USA
BVRC100829250422
635251BV00003B/25